THE GNOME WITH THE KNOBBLY KNEES

Other books about
Joe, Laurie and Theo

1. The Dog in the Diamond Collar
'A proper story, entertainingly observed.'
Sunday Times

2. The Boy in the Big Black Box
*'Full of highly satisfactory twists
and entertaining magic.'*
The Best New Books for Children – Guardian

By the same author
Dogs Don't Do Dishes
Toad Prince

And for older readers
Copper
Amethyst

THE GNOME WITH THE KNOBBLY KNEES

REBECCA LISLE

Illustrated by Tim Archbold

ANDERSEN PRESS · LONDON

To Bella Russell Heller – RL

To Rosie and John – TA

First published in 2009
by Andersen Press Limited
20 Vauxhall Bridge Road
London SW1V 2SA
www.andersenpress.co.uk
www.rebeccalisle.com

This edition published in 2014

Text copyright © Rebecca Lisle, 2009
Illustration copyright © Tim Archbold, 2009

British Library Cataloguing in Publication Data available.

ISBN 978 184 270 889 7

Printed and bound in China

1
In the Garden Next Door

Clinky Monkey did not want to go through the hedge. He dug in his toes; he whined and whimpered. Joe, the eldest and biggest of the three boys, had to carry him through. 'Scaredy cat!' he said.

'Scaredy *dog*, you mean,' Laurie said. 'That dog doesn't deserve to wear a diamond collar!'

'He does. He's the Best Dog in the Whole World,' said Theo, the littlest brother.

'You know, if we sold that collar we could buy a million best dogs in the world,' said Laurie.

Theo shook his head. 'Uh uh. Never.'

The boys were going through the hedge to the garden next door. The house had been empty for years. The grass was waist high, weeds choked the roses; dark creepers crept over the walls and railings.

'It's spooky. It feels like we're being watched,' Laurie said.

Clinky Monkey agreed; for once he stayed close and did not need to be told to *heel*.

'What now, Joe?' Laurie said. 'It was your great idea to come here.'

'We'll explore,' said Joe, straightening his explorer's hat. 'Go on, Theo. You first.'

They inched towards the gloomy house. Everything was still and silent . . . until suddenly Clinky Monkey started barking.

'Woof! Woof! Woof! Woof!'

'Clinky is so daft! Now he's scared of a bush!' Joe said.

'If Clinky says there's something wrong with that bush, there is,' Theo said. 'He is the Cleverest Dog in the Whole World.'

Joe pushed the leaves aside. 'Well, well,' he said, 'look here.'

'Clinky's right for once,' Laurie said. 'He's sniffed out a funny garden gnome.'

'Goody. I've *always* wanted a garden gnome,' Theo said.

The gnome was nearly as big as little Theo. He was wearing a green jacket and blue trousers. His hat was yellow. He had a white beard and squinty sky blue eyes. His knees were very knobbly.

Joe crouched down beside it. 'I've never seen a gnome with a *yellow* hat before,' Joe said. 'Hmm . . . See how shiny he is? No scratches or dust. I think he's brand new. *Weird.'*

All three boys slowly turned and stared at the house. They were all thinking the same thought.

Was there someone in the house after all?

'There's a face at the window!' Laurie cried.

'Face ahoy!' Theo roared.

'Run-for-it!' Joe yelled.

They raced back to the hole in the hedge and home.

2
Clinky Monkey Gets a Visitor

Later, while the boys ate lunch, Clinky Monkey settled down in his garden to chew a smelly trainer. He was having a gloriously slobbery time . . . until he looked up. There, not a tail's length away, right beside the wheelbarrow, was the garden gnome with the knobbly knees.

Clinky was up on his toes instantly. 'Yeroooowf!' he howled as he walked backwards. 'Yerwoof!' Never taking his eyes from the garden gnome, he backed all the way up the garden until he backed into Joe and knocked him over.

'Ouch! What's the matter, Clinky?'

Clinky Monkey circled Joe, yapping nervously. He ran down the lawn towards the wheelbarrow, looking behind him all the time. *Come on! Come on!*

'I'm coming – whoops!' Joe got up and tripped over a rabbit. They had two identical white rabbits and this was one of them. 'Everyone wants to trip me up! Were you barking at Rabbit?' Joe asked. 'You aren't scared of *Rabbit,* are you?'

But Clinky Monkey wasn't listening.

He was circling the wheelbarrow slowly, looking more and more puzzled.

The garden gnome had vanished.

3
Disguises

The boys were up in their tree house, the Bed of Luck, from where they could see into the next door's garden.

'Can you see any sign of anyone?' Laurie said.

'No, I'm sure it's empty,' Joe said. 'You just imagined you saw a face.'

'Didn't *you* see anyone at the window, Theo?'

'No, but I will say I did if you want me to,' said Theo kindly.

'Ignore him,' Joe said. 'He'll say anything.'

'Anything?' Theo said.

'See? He's a dimwit!'

'He can't help it,' said Joe. 'Now, concentrate. We have a mystery to investigate.'

'Great!' Laurie said. 'We'll need disguises! No one must know we're the boys from next door.'

'Let's be girls then,' Theo said.

'Girls! *Beough!*' Laurie made a disgusted face. 'We can't be *girls!* Anyway, *you* can't come. You always forget you're disguised and do something silly. Remember when we dressed up as cats – you kept barking.'

'I *can* come. You *have* to take me. Mum says—'

'Actually,' Joe said, 'Theo might just have said something clever for once.'

'No, I don't think I did,' Theo said.

'Girls is a good idea,' Joe said. 'Who'd imagine boys would ever be mad enough to dress up as silly girls?'

So they got dressed up.

Theo chose his mum's lacy pink nightie. Joe wore a sunhat with roses on and a pink T-shirt that said GIRLS ARE MADE

OF SUGAR & SPICE. Laurie wore his mum's sundress and high-heeled shoes. They smeared their lips with the reddest lipstick they could find.

'No one will recognise us like this!' Joe said.

As they stepped outside, Liz, the young woman who lived opposite, walked past. 'Hello, boys,' Liz said, laughing. 'Love the costumes! Are you going to a fancy dress party?'

'Ignore her,' Joe said, going the colour of Ribena. 'Let her laugh.'

'We don't have to *let* her,' Laurie hissed. 'She's doing it all on her own!'

The house next door was set back from the lane and surrounded by a scabby wooden fence. The three boy/girls tugged the gate open, pushed past the rubbery, dusty bushes that crowded the path and went up to the front door.

The shutters were pulled across the ground floor windows. There were letters spewing out of the letterbox in the door.

'See, it's empty,' Joe whispered. 'You ring the bell, Laurie.'

'*You* ring the bell,' Laurie said.

'You ring it. *You* said you saw someone.'

'You do it.'

'You.'

'Theo, ring the doorbell!'

'Brrrrrrrrring!'

Clinky Monkey barked. He always barked when a doorbell went. OK, so it wasn't his doorbell, but he'd give it a good telling off anyway. 'Woof, woof, woof!'

'Shut up!' the boys yelled at him.

The door did not open. Nothing stirred inside the house.

'I told you no one lives here,' Joe said. 'The garden is safe to play in.'

But as Laurie turned back to fasten the gate shut, a sudden movement at an upper window caught his eye.

He looked up: a bald-headed man wearing tinted round glasses slipped quickly back out of view.

4
Clinky Monkey
Receives Another Visit

Night-time.

Clinky Monkey was asleep, curled up in his basket in the kitchen.

Suddenly he snapped awake. His ears pricked up; he had heard something.

He stared towards the cat flap. It was flapping backwards and forwards with a *click-clack* noise. He glanced over at the cat's basket: the cat was snoring.

Clinky Monkey sat up very, very slowly. His hackles rose. A growl started up in the depths of his belly, rumbled round his ribs and rattled in his throat. He bared his teeth and faced the door.

The cat flap was being lifted up from the outside. It opened slowly, slowly.

A thin beam of torchlight shone straight through the square hole and into the kitchen. The diamonds on Clinky Monkey's collar sparkled like stars.

A small face appeared in the cat flap. Two sky-blue eyes stared straight in.

The garden gnome!

Woofwoofwoofwoof!

Clinky Monkey dashed at the cat flap. He snapped. He growled. He howled. He barked and barked until Joe came down to see what the matter was. Joe was wearing his jimjams and a baseball hat.

Yawning, Joe patted Clinky Monkey's head. 'What's up, Clinky?'

'Woofwoofwoofwoofwoof!'

'What? There's nothing here. It's all right. Want to go out for a wee?'

'Woofwoofwoofwoof.'

'Shush! All right, out you go.'

Joe opened the back door but Clinky Monkey didn't want to go out. He peered out into the blackness. He wasn't going out into the night, not when the peculiar little garden gnome with the knobbly knees was out there . . .

Waiting!

5
The Great Gnome Giveaway

On Saturday the boys walked into the village to buy their Saturday sweets.

A new shop had opened:

GRIBBLE'S GARDEN STORES

Outside it were heaps of garden things; wheelbarrows, pots, spades, plants and bags of compost. And ...

Garden gnomes!

The gnomes all wore blue trousers and green jackets. They all had beards and yellow hats with bells.

A notice said:

GRIBBLES' GNOMES FOR HOMES!

A GNOME IN THE HOME IS WORTH TWO IN A BUSH. HOURS OF ENJOYMENT AND PLEASURE!

MAKE A GNOME HAPPY TODAY AND TAKE ONE HOME!

A woman with hard-looking blonde hair and glittering earrings came out of the shop carrying one of the garden gnomes.

'Isn't he cute?' she said to the boys. 'He's an indoor gnome. And he was free!'

Then a man walked out of the shop. He wore a flash suit and a diamond twinkled on his tie.

'I only went in to buy a packet of seeds,' he said, 'and Mr Gribble threw in this gnome, playing a flute, for free! I'm going to put him in my music room!'

'That gnome should have a fiddle,' Joe said, but the man had gone. 'Garden gnomes don't play the flute. They play the fiddle. Or they fish. It's not right.'

'Let's go get one if they're free,' Laurie said. 'I want one – even if it's got a broken foot like that one had.'

'I've *always* wanted a home gnome,' Theo said.

They went into the shop.

Mr Gribble was so small he had to stand on an upturned wheelbarrow behind the counter. He glared at the three boys.

Laurie squeezed Joe's arm tight. 'Joe—' he whispered.

'Shh!' Joe said.

It was too late to go back.

'A packet of seeds please,' Joe said to Mr Gribble. 'Or anything really, really cheap, like no more than 20p.'

'Go away,' said Mr Gribble.

'But we want to b—'

'Hop it, you lot!'

The three boys stood very still and did not hop it. It was an unwritten rule never to hop it or skedaddle or clear off when told to and they weren't about to break that rule now.

'What are you staring at? I told you to hop it!' the man shouted.

'Rabbits hop,' Joe said.

'We aren't rabbits,' Theo said, thoughtfully. 'But we do have two rabbits. Rabbit and Rabbit. They don't look at all like us – well, a bit like Joe. Are your glasses working?'

Joe gazed at Theo with admiration. He could never tell whether his little brother was being rude or dumb or funny or all three.

Mr Gribble looked like he suspected Theo of being all three. He took a yellow hanky from the pocket of his green waistcoat and rubbed his little round glasses with it. Then he spun round and stared fiercely at the boys.

'Don't I know you?' he said. 'I've seen you before!'

'We're on the telly,' said Laurie, thinking quickly. 'We're famous. We're the Three Sweet Simpering Sisters. You probably recognise us from our show.'

'You're *boys*!'

'Mum says girls are as clever as boys,' Theo said.

Laurie shook his head gravely. 'We're in disguise!' he said. He beamed at Mr Gribble as if Mr Gribble were an idiot. 'We're *im-per-son-a-ting* boys,' he said very slowly.

Mr Gribble looked like he'd taken a bite of a lemon. 'Go and impersonate an empty space. Clear off!'

'Keep your hair on,' Joe said.

Mr Gribble automatically felt his bald head. 'Cheeky!' He threw a tulip bulb at them. It missed. 'Hey! Keep still while I throw things at you!' He jumped off the barrow and hopped onto the counter. He really was very short. Not much taller than little Theo. He picked up a plant pot and held it above his head ready to throw. 'Skedaddle!' he yelled.

The boys skedaddled.

'What a horrid, horrid man,' Laurie said.

'Probably got personal problems,' Joe said.

'I don't want a gnome anyway,' Theo said, 'not one that blinks.'

'Which gnome blinks?'

'That one!' Theo pointed at a gnome sitting reading a book. 'And he's got six fingers.'

'Gnomes don't blink. You imagined it,' said Joe. 'They shouldn't read books either. Or wear yellow hats. Gnomes should have red hats. It's just not right.'

'Hush! Listen, you two. Bad news,' said Laurie. 'Mr Gribble was the man I saw in the empty house – Gribble is our next-door neighbour!'

6
Clinky Monkey
Gets a Third Visit

Clinky Monkey wouldn't settle down in his own basket in the kitchen and no one knew why. He wouldn't even stay in the kitchen. He wanted to be upstairs. Theo's bedroom door was shut, so he fell asleep on Laurie's bed instead.

The bedroom window was open. The curtains were slightly parted so moonlight shone in, casting a long silver line across the floor, like a spotlight.

Suddenly the curtains moved. There was a soft rattling sound.

Clinky Monkey was awake in seconds.

A tiny hand was pushing the window open. A little man was squeezing into the room . . .

The garden gnome with the knobbly knees!

Clinky Monkey stayed as still as a rock. Beneath his half-closed eyes his eyeballs swivelled like ball bearings as he watched the intruder.

The gnome balanced on the windowsill and looked around, then dropped silently to the floor with a soft grunt. He tiptoed across the carpet following the moonlight strip right up to Laurie's bed.

He carefully climbed up the end of the bed and crossed the covers, his tiny feet sinking silently into the white duvet as if it were snow.

Clinky Monkey waited until the gnome was only three inches away, then he opened his jaws and dived. *Snap!* The gnome was caught.

'What – what's happening?' Laurie sprang awake. The dog and gnome stayed completely rigid; like a frozen frame in a film. Laurie slithered up to the top end of the bed and hugged his pillow. 'Crikey!'

'Tell your dog to let go!' squeaked the gnome.

'Who said that? Did *you* say that?'

'Yes.'

'Garden gnomes don't talk!' said Laurie.

'This one does.'

'It does? You do! Great! Fantastic! Hang on . . . Don't move! Clinky Monkey, stay! Hold on tight! Got to get the others. I'll be right back!'

He came back seconds later with Joe and Theo. Joe rubbed his eyes and stared. Theo rubbed his eyes and stared.

'I can't believe it!' Joe said.

'You can. Just try.'

'I'm trying,' Theo said. 'I'm trying really hard.'

'OK.' Joe sat down on Laurie's bed and stared at the dog and the gnome. 'I believe it.'

Theo patted Clinky Monkey. 'Well done, Clinky!' he said. 'You captured an intruder! You are the Best Guard Dog in the Whole World!'

Clinky Monkey's tail *thump, thumped* on the duvet. He kept his jaws locked tightly around the gnome's leg.

Suddenly there was the crackle and hiss of radio noises. The boys jumped. They looked round the room.

'What was that?'

'Flipping fungi! Excuse me,' said the gnome. He gave the bell on the top of his hat a little twist. To the boys' amazement torch light streamed out from it, radiating in a circle around the gnome's head. 'Bit dark in here,' the gnome squeaked. He pressed the top button on his fat tummy. 'Won't be a sec.' He pulled out the second button, which was on a long, coiled wire and spoke into it. 'Receiving you loud and clear,' he said.

'You're LATE!' A voice blared out. It was Mr Gribble.

7
What a Good
Garden Gnome Longs For

'You're late!' Mr Gribble shouted. 'Any problems?'

The gnome looked down at Clinky Monkey's sharp teeth clamped around his leg. 'No problems at all, not at all,' the gnome whimpered. 'Quarry's in sight; very close in fact.'

'Hurry up! You're so slow! Over and OUT!'

'Er, goodbye.' The gnome let go of the button and it went spinning and whirring back into place. He twiddled with his bell and the torch light faded. 'Oh, dear,' he sighed. 'Oh, dearie dear.'

'Cool hat,' said Joe. 'Wish mine did that.'

'What are you doing in my bedroom?' Laurie said. 'And what's your *quarry*?'

'I'll tell you, only, could you ask your dog to take his teeth out of me?' said the gnome in a trembling voice. 'I'm attached to that leg.'

'No,' Theo said.

'Please. I promise I won't run,' said the gnome.

'First tell us what you're doing here,' Joe asked him.

The gnome sighed. 'I'm stealing Clinky Monkey's collar,' he said. 'That's what I'm doing.'

Clinky Monkey gulped. He almost lost his grip on the gnome.

'You're a *thief*!' Theo said. 'You want *our* diamond collar?'

The gnome sighed again. 'It's the Great Gnome Robbery,' he said. 'Mr Gribble is the brains; I'm just a cog in his great thieving machinery. My name is ZE3.' A tear rolled down his face. 'I want to be a good gnome, not a bad gnome with one leg.'

'I think he's telling the truth,' Laurie said.

'So do I.' Joe got up and shut the door and the window.

'OK,' Theo said. 'Drop him, Clinky Monkey. Drop!'

Clinky Monkey dropped him. He crinkled up his lips and wiped his muzzle on the duvet cover. *Beough*, gnomes!

'You see,' said ZE3, 'all Gribble's gnomes are rejects. If you look closely you'll see I have extremely knobbly knees.' He pointed at his knees.

'You're right,' Joe said. 'I can see that without even looking closely.'

'Gribble took us from the discard heap at the gnome factory. He makes us wear these yellow hats and the hats make us rob and steal and plunder . . . but I'm not very good at it.'

Nobody disagreed with him.

'Can't you just take the hat off?' Joe said, reaching to remove it.

'No!' squeaked ZE3. 'We—'

But Joe had already pulled off the hat. ZE3 went cross-eyed, muttered something about goldfish, and toppled over.

'Whoops!' Joe said.

Theo picked up the hat and looked inside it. There were green, red and blue wires in the lining. 'Look!'

'They must re-route the nerve impulses in the brain,' Joe said. 'A dastardly plan!'

Laurie and Theo looked at Joe in amazement. 'Joe! You just made that up!'

'Ha, ha! Sounds clever though!'

'Look at his neck,' said Laurie. 'He's got the name Soppy Sam printed on it.'

'I wonder if that's his real name and not ZE3?' said Joe. 'Better put his hat back on, Theo.'

ZE3 came to life again once his hat was on. He had absolutely no memory of what had just occurred, and went on talking as if nothing had happened.

'Gribble's plan is to give us away in his garden shop, not as *garden gnomes*,' said ZE3, 'but *home* gnomes for inside the house—'

'He wouldn't give us one,' Joe said.

'He only gives them away to rich people! So we can get inside the rich person's house. As soon as the rich person is asleep, we pinch things. I can spot a diamond at four hundred paces – sad, isn't it?'

'Well, it could be useful,' Theo said. 'If Clinky Monkey lost a diamond from his collar for example. Can you teach me?'

'I don't want to be useful!' squeaked ZE3.

'Does the name Soppy Sam mean anything to you?' Joe asked him.

'Soppy Sam? *Soppy Sam?*' The gnome tapped his chin thoughtfully. 'No, I don't think so. Why?'

'Nothing.'

'I don't want to be a robber,' went on ZE3. 'I don't want to be a Home Gnome.'

'What do you want to be then?'

'Just a sweet, ornamental, ordinary, useless garden gnome,' said ZE3, smiling dreamily. 'An ordinary garden gnome in a pretty garden, doing ordinary garden gnome things like . . .'

'Sitting on a toadstool?' Joe said.

'Pushing a wheelbarrow nowhere?' Laurie suggested.

'Fishing into thin air?' Theo said.

'Crikey, a gnome life's not very exciting, is it?' Laurie said.

'It's heaven!' sobbed ZE3, wiping a tear from his eye. 'But we aren't allowed to have it: no gardens for us because we weren't perfect. We are good gnomes, longing for the life of an ordinary garden gnome. Gribble saved us from the scrapheap but all he's given us is a career in night-dark robbery!'

'Yeah, I'd like a gnome's lifestyle,' Joe said. 'Fishing, dreaming, wheelbarrowing – much better than school.'

'Gribble plans to disappear tomorrow with all the stolen treasures,' said ZE3 with a sigh. 'Nobody can stop Gribble.'

'Oh, we can,' Theo said.

'Yeah, we'll think of something,' Joe said. 'Will you help us?'

The gnome nodded. 'But it won't be easy, Gribble is *so* blooming clever!'

'Don't worry. We're cleverer and smarterer,' Joe told him. 'You are no longer a gnome alone!'

8
Greedy Gribble

Gribble sat on a high stool in his cobwebby attic room. Laid out before him were diamond rings, gold bracelets, necklaces of precious stones, jewel-encrusted watches. A fortune!

A one-eared gnome scuttled in. He laid a purple velvet bundle on the desk. 'Silver spoons,' he squeaked.

'Good work, ZB4!' Gribble examined the spoons. He wrote in his notebook:

Six silver teaspoons
1920 Birmingham

'Now, turn round.'

The obedient gnome was trembling as he turned round. If Gribble saw the little gnome's shivers, he ignored them.

Gribble eased off the gnome's yellow hat. 'Nighty-night!'

'I do miss just sitting around in the garden,' the gnome said weakly.

'Shut up, you little squirt. And don't mention gardens!'

'I – wish – sometimes,' said ZB4 slowly, 'we – could—' He was sinking to his knees.

'Shut up.'

'. . . go – fish – ing – and—' ZB4 slowly keeled over onto the floor with a soft thud.

Gribble opened a drawer full of yellow hats. He stuffed ZB4's in with them. Then he kicked the gnome across the attic. ZB4 bounced across the floorboards into the pile of other deactivated gnomes in the corner.

'Ow! I shouldn't have done that!' said Gribble, biting his knuckles. 'I shouldn't have done that! Bad Gribble! But why should *you* have a good life if I can't?' he growled. 'We all want to fish. We all want to play the fiddle in the last rays of the dying sun. See dawn spreading over the emerald lawn. But we can't! We can't!' He drummed his fingers on the desk. 'Curses! Curses! Hurry up, ZE3!'

At last he heard small footsteps scampering up the wooden stairs.

'You're late, Knobbly Knees!' Gribble yelled. He scowled at the little gnome. 'Well?' He held out his hand. 'The diamond collar? Where is it, you dummy?'

'I couldn't—' squeaked ZE3. 'The dog was too fierce, and—'

'Too fierce?'

44

'Yes. Look.' The gnome showed him Clinky Monkey's teeth marks in his leg. 'See? Dearie me, he was a massive hound! As big as a reindeer. But I've found something better!'

Mr Gribble's little round eyes grew as hard as marbles. He took off his glasses, polished them with a yellow hanky and focused his eyes on ZE3. 'Explain.'

'I overheard the boys next door, talking. They've found a hoard of money!'

'Go on!' Gribble's blue eyes went squinty with greed.

'A suitcase full of used fifty pound notes! Trillions! And they don't know what to do with it.'

Mr Gribble slapped his hand on the desk so the jewellery jumped up, shimmering like thousands of tiny leaping fish. 'They don't know what to do with trillions of pounds?'

'No, they're only young. They've hidden it.'

'And you know where it's hidden?'

'Yes. And of course I'm not strong enough to carry back a whole suitcase of money. You'll have to come and get it.'

Mr Gribble licked his lips and rolled his eyes.

'Trillions of quid! Ah haaa! Let's go now!' Gribble stood up and pulled his green waistcoat neatly into place. 'Come on!'

'No, not now,' said ZE3, quickly. 'It's locked up at night. Tomorrow. I'll need to go to the boys' house in the morning and make sure they're busy – we don't want to run into them there – then I'll show you where it is.'

It was a lie. It was all a lie.

The reason ZE3 had to wait for daylight was so that Theo would be up because Theo was at the centre of the amazing plan.

9
Greedy Theo

Laid out on Theo's bedroom floor next morning, were a yellow pointed hat, a green jacket, blue trousers, and a false grey beard.

'It's a garden gnome outfit. Fantastic, isn't it, Theo?' Joe said. He was unwrapping a bar of chocolate as he spoke.

'I don't want to be a ga—'

Joe shoved a square of chocolate into his mouth. 'You have to!'

'Bub you bed I wab no good at drebbing up, you bed . . .' Theo mumbled.

'*That* was different. That was then. *This* is now.'

Theo loved chocolate. He could eat four big bars of chocolate, or eight small bars of chocolate or twelve chocolate

Christmas decorations in one go without being sick; it was tried and tested.

Theo put the clothes on. He looked just like a garden gnome, a bit taller than little ZE3, but not much.

'Good boy!' Laurie patted his head.

'We're going to play a trick,' Joe said. 'And it won't work without you. You are important.'

'I don't want—'

'Yes, you do,' Joe stuck more chocolate in his mouth. 'And,' he went on, 'Laurie is going to give you all his next week's sweetie money and I will give you all my next week's sweetie money if you do this, OK? Have some more chocolate.'

Theo chewed thoughtfully. 'All of it?'

'Yes. And if you *don't* do this very small favour for your dear brothers ... well, what sort of a little brother are you?' Laurie said. 'You're a baby brother who doesn't care for his big brothers at all. Doesn't want his big brothers to be proud of him or—'

'I'll do it.'

'Right. Now here's the plan ...'

10
Gribble Runs Around

Next morning Mr Gribble crouched on a box beside his attic window watching for ZE3 to appear from the boys' house next door. When he did, Gribble would know the three boys were out of the way and he and ZE3 could go and get the money. He was so excited his glasses were steaming up. He was picturing piles of used pound notes, heaps, *mountains* of money waiting for him! He was so excited he almost didn't see the little gnome when he appeared in the garden below.

'Stupid little twerp!' he cursed. 'I nearly missed him!'

Gribble sprinted down the stairs and out of the house through the coal chute. Not for one moment did Gribble imagine that the garden gnome he was following was anyone other than ZE3.

He was in such a hurry he got in a tangle with his gate and caught his trousers. 'Curses!' he muttered, hearing the fabric rip. A flash of blue showed underneath his trousers. 'Double curses!'

By the time Gribble was free, ZE3 was far ahead, running down the lane.

'Slow down, you silly twit,' Gribble said. 'I can't run that fast! What's the hurry, the money's not going anywhere, is it? Pound notes don't have legs!' He chuckled. Pound notes with legs! That would be funny.

Gribble ran.

The gnome squeezed through the

hedge that circled the allotments. Gribble got in a tangle with the prickly hedge when he tried to get through. The thorns caught hold of his jacket and he struggled and fought. The only way to get free was by leaving his jacket behind; he had a green one underneath.

The allotments were deserted, but even so, Gribble took care to keep behind the bushes and the sheds as he followed ZE3's bright yellow hat. The garden gnome was speeding along, weaving in and out of clusters of pea sticks, dodging spiky roses and leaping rows of cabbages.

'Where is ZE3 going?' Gribble muttered to himself. 'Where *is* the money hidden?'

ZE3 went through a muddy bed of potatoes. He zigzagged through some plum trees and set a whole load of wasps buzzing angrily. He went behind a fence, under some low bushes, right through a pond.

'Why doesn't he stop? Why's he going so fast? Since when did ZE3 have such sprinting legs?' Gribble wondered. He was so busy watching the gnome that he tripped over a rake and fell flat on his face. 'Curses! Curses!'

He got up and a twig spiked his bald head. 'Curses!' Now the gnome was right on the other side of the allotment, heading for the woods. 'I shan't *only* deactivate ZE3 after this,' he told himself. 'I'll jolly well rip off his head, tear off his nose and mangle his yellow hat!'

11
Yellow Hats and Red Hats

Meanwhile Joe and Laurie were putting the next part of their plan into action.

While Gribble was chasing the other 'gnome' around the allotments, the *real* ZE3 had opened up the coal chute for them and now they were inside the house next door. There were no light bulbs so ZE3 turned on his hat-torch and lit everything up.

The first thing they saw when they opened the attic door was the heap of hatless bald gnomes piled higgledy-piggledy in the corner. Their sky-blue eyes gazed sightlessly at the ceiling.

'Poor precious things!' squeaked ZE3. 'A tragedy – he's taken their hats!'

'Where's he hidden them?' Laurie began

searching. 'We must put them back on.'

'Here they are!' ZE3 cried, opening the drawer. Joe picked up a gnome and pulled a yellow hat over his bald head. The gnome twitched into life.

'Silver – gold – diamonds—' he muttered flatly.

Joe pushed the hat on more firmly: the gnome started to wave his legs and arms wildly. 'Must find gold. Must get money. Rob. Rob. Rob. Steal. Gribble's home gnome. A *plant* in your house, hee hee.'

'Yes, you were right, ZE3, it's all in the hat!' Joe took the hat off again and the gnome fell lifelessly to the floor. 'Glad none of my hats work like that!'

'Dearie me!' cried ZE3. 'Trembling toadstools! We can't live *without* our hats and we can't live *with* them! We're doomed! Doomed!' He began to weep.

We're doomed!

But Joe and Laurie had already got an idea. They began to search the dusty cupboards and boxes.

'What are you looking for?' ZE3 asked.

'The proper hats! *Red* hats,' said Joe. 'I always said that garden gnomes should have red hats! Ah ha!' he cried. 'Just as I thought!' He held up a bag of Mighty Big Super Grow All Purpose Compost.

'Compost?' ZE3 said tearfully. 'Why would we—?'

Joe turned the bag upside down and red hats tumbled out like autumn leaves.

'Dearie me,' ZE3 said, dabbing his eyes. 'A sight for sore eyes. I do love red.'

ZE3 picked up a red hat. 'Look, they've got names in them,' he said. 'Didn't you say something about ... *Soppy Sam*?'

'We did. Why don't you put it on?' Laurie said.

But as soon as the gnome took off the yellow hat, he crashed, insensible to the floor.

'Poor thing!' Laurie said, propping him up against the chair. 'I'm sure this is his hat – Soppy Sam is a perfect name for him.'

Laurie put the red hat on ZE3. Immediately the gnome jumped up. he skipped round the room singing a song about bumblebees and butterflies.

'It was his hat all right,' Joe said.

The boys looked at the other hats: Dippy Dave, Bigfoot…

'Oh, they're going to be so happy when they get these and remember everything!' Soppy Sam cried.

'Stop dancing and help!' Joe said. 'Gribble might come back at any moment!'

They began red-hatting the gnomes. Each gnome had their name on their necks. With the correct hat on, the gnome came to life and started whistling or singing, laughing and dancing round the room.

'Fishing, I — *love* — fishing . . . ' the gnome called Squiffy trilled like a budgie.

'I love to go a-wandering along the mountain track,' sang Bigfoot stamping round the room on his giant feet.

'One hat left,' Joe said, waving it around. 'It's a bit bigger, this one. Got the name *Beanpole* printed inside. Does that ring a bell?'

The gnomes shook their heads. They didn't know who Beanpole was.

Soppy Sam rounded up the gnomes. 'Listen. Last night you took something valuable from your homes and—'

The gnomes burst out shouting. They turned on Soppy Sam shaking their fists at him.

'No!'

'I couldn't do that!'

'I'm an honest gnome!'

'I'd never steal. I've been brought up proper.'

'It's a lie! I wouldn't!'

'Hush, hush!' Joe cried above the racket. 'I'm glad you've forgotten – the theft was an accident and easy to put right. I have a list here of what you, er, *borrowed*.' Joe waved Gribble's list in the air. 'You just have to return what you stole to its rightful owner. No one will notice. Then you're free to go and sit in the garden—'

'In the *garden*?'

'Can I fish all day long by a concrete pond?'

'Can I sit cross-legged on a red and white toadstool?'

'Can I just stare and stare and stare?'

'Yes, yes,' Soppy Sam said.

'Lush!'

'Don't just stand there all dreamy!' Laurie said. 'Get going!'

'You don't want to be here when Gribble comes back!' Soppy Sam said. 'We're free from Gribble for ever!'

Quickly the gnomes lined up. As Laurie read out the list of precious things, each gnome was given the item he had taken. They still couldn't believe they'd been bad. Some of them were crying.

'To think I stole this!'

'Me? A common thief! What would my dear mother say?'

'You never had a mother,' said Laurie.

'Yes, I did! Are you calling me a liar?'

'But you came from a factory!'

'So what? I believe I had a mother and she loved me.'

Joe shrugged. 'I suppose we all need a mother,' he said.

The gnomes stuffed the stolen jewellery, watches and money into their clothing and under their hats. Laughing they ran off to put it back in their homes.

'But what will happen when they get back?' Joe asked. 'Won't their owners see they're alive?'

Soppy Sam chuckled. 'Did you ever see a gnome move before?'

'No.'

'We like humans around,' said Soppy Sam, 'and we'd never want to frighten them by moving.'

'We should get taught useful stuff like that at school,' Laurie said. 'I could come top of a Garden Gnome exam.'

'We'd better go and look for Theo, now,' Joe said. 'He's only little and Gribble is big and mean.'

'Theo won't let him catch him,' Laurie said. 'He's too smart! He's the smartest little brother I know.'

Suddenly a door banged loudly. A man shouted up the stairs.

It was Gribble!

Everyone froze.

'Uh oh!'

'Hide!'

Joe and Laurie nipped behind the door. Soppy Sam didn't move. He couldn't move; he was stunned, like a rabbit caught in the glare of car headlights.

12
Gribble Gets Confused

While the boys and ZE3 had been searching Gribble's room, the *other* ZE3 had run three times around the allotment, through the woods, over the river, round the playground and then back through the allotment again. Three times Gribble had followed him. Finally, limping, dirty, scratched and very angry, Gribble had come to a dead end — a small old shed in the corner of a bed of broad beans. It had to be the end of the chase — there was nowhere else the gnome could have gone.

'At last!' Gribble cried, approaching the shed. 'I'm going to mangle you, ZE3!'

He crashed the door open against the wall. 'Where's my money!'

But there was no gnome inside the shed. No suitcase. No trillions of pounds. There was just a small boy in a green jacket sitting on an upturned box, swinging his legs and eating a bar of chocolate. Beside him sat a black and white dog wearing a yellow hat and a false beard. The dog jumped at him, barking.

Gribble stood in the doorway open-mouthed.

'Where's ZE3? Where's the money?' He looked round wildly. 'Hey!' he added as Clinky Monkey snapped at him. 'Keep that dog back, keep him back!'

'Hello,' the little boy said sweetly. 'Lovely weather for the time of year. Did you go for a walk to get some fresh hair – I mean *air*?'

'What? Why? Who are you anyway?' Gribble spluttered. 'Don't I know you?'

'No, you don't know me,' said Theo. 'I think you'd better go, or my dog will bite your leg clean off in one snap! He can. I've seen him do it before. He likes biting off hands too. And noses. And—'

'There's something fishy going on,' Gribble interrupted. 'Something's fishy. It's not right!'

Clinky Monkey had had enough. He wasn't having any short-legged, squinty-eyed baldy shouting at his Theo. He charged. Gribble turned and ran. The leash slipped from Theo's hand and Clinky Monkey just managed to eat the seat of Gribble's trousers before he leaped out of the door.

Beneath his brown trousers, Gribble wore a *blue* pair.

13
Beanpole's Red Hat

Now Gribble was back at his house, and Laurie and Joe were trapped, hiding behind the attic door.

Gribble slammed the front door shut. 'ZE3! You are a worthless wired-up nitwit!' he roared as he tramped up the stairs. 'I'm going to tear you limb from limb! I'm going to twist off your nose! I'm going to—'

ZE3/Soppy Sam stood rooted to the spot, shivering like a jelly.

Gribble burst in. He was wearing a green jacket and blue trousers. He had lost his round glasses and his sky blue eyes were strangely squinty. He had turned his yellow hanky into a yellow hat.

Soppy Sam gasped. 'Well, eat my mouldy

mushrooms! You're a garden gnome!' he cried. 'I see it all now!' He held up the spare red hat. 'This is *your* hat! *You* are Beanpole!'

With a roar, Gribble lunged at Soppy Sam.

'No!' Laurie quickly stuck out his leg. Gribble tripped over it and went sprawling across the floor.

'Jump on him!' Joe yelled. They jumped on Gribble and pinned him to the floor so he couldn't move.

Written on the back of his neck was the word Beanpole.

'We know everything,' Laurie told him. 'No point in fighting. We know the secret of the yellow hats. We've freed the gnomes. It's over!'

'No! No!' Gribble cried, kicking his little legs against the floor. 'It's not fair! No!'

'You're a gnome!' Soppy Sam cried. 'How could you do this to your fellow gnomes?'

'Let go of me! Get off! I'll snip off your ears with secateurs! I'll dig you into the earth and feed you to the worms!'

'Temper, temper.' Joe winked at Laurie and together they slipped off his yellow hat. 'Got you!' they cried.

They'd expected Gribble to blank out and his eyes to glaze over like boiled eggs. But that didn't happen.

Gribble snapped: 'Of course I'm not a gnome! Get off me!'

Joe, Laurie and Soppy Sam got off him.

'Well, you look like a garden gnome,' said Joe.

'I am not a garden gnome!' Gribble shouted. 'I wish I were! I'd love to be a gnome. I'd make a perfect garden gnome. Perfect.'

'So what's going on?' Joe asked him.

Gribble sighed. 'I suppose I have to tell you . . .'

'I used to work in Grimshaw's Garden Gnome Factory,' he said. 'I loved my work. I took such care and time over each little fellow I made! Each of my gnomes was a miracle.'

'What went wrong?' Laurie asked.

Gribble collapsed like a bag of compost, a tear dribbled down his cheek. 'I started dressing like my gnomes. I grew a beard like the gnomes. I went fishing, I took up the fiddle. I wanted to *be* a gnome. And the other workers at the factory laughed at me! They called me Beanpole. They made that hat for me. They even wrote my name on my neck with permanent ink. They said I was a reject! A loser! They said I was mad!'

'Yes.' Laurie and Joe nodded. 'Absolutely.'

'You think I'm mad?'

'Oh, no, no!'

'I decided to get my own back on them,' said Gribble. 'I gathered up the rejects; gnomes too small, too fat, big feet, knobbly knees, squiffy noses, and made them those yellow hats and special jackets.

Then I sent them off thieving and – well – you know the rest.'

'You've been cruel to us,' Soppy Sam said. 'Treated us badly.'

'I know. I see now, I've become bitter and twisted.'

'If you really want to be a garden gnome,' Joe said, 'why don't you just go out into the garden or the park or something and sit there and be one?'

'I'm too big.'

'Ah, so you are. Big but small.'

'What can I do?'

Laurie thought a bit. 'You should go into business selling odd and peculiar garden gnomes,' he said. 'You could collect all the rejects up from Grimshaw's factory if they don't want them and sell them as specialities. *Give a sad gnome a home.*'

'That is brilliant!' Gribble cried, leaping up. 'A wonderful idea!'

'And if you dressed like a gnome,' said Joe, 'being so vertically challenged, and everything, that would be a great gimmick – you'd make a fortune. Legally.'

Gribble grinned. 'It's a brilliant idea. I'm going to start straight away!' He jigged around, anxious to leave. 'I'm going to have such a wonderful time! And be so rich! And everyone will love me!' Then he ran. 'Goodbye!'

They heard him chortling and cheering as he bounded down the stairs.

'Phew! Sorted,' Joe said. 'Another great mystery solved.'

Laurie was turning a hat round in his hands. 'I wonder what would happen if I put one of these on?' Laurie said.

'Oh, no you don't!' Joe pushed the desk drawer shut tightly. 'One little imp is enough in the family, thank you.'

'Who *do* you mean?' Laurie said.

* * *

Theo was waiting for them in the Bed of Luck. 'You were ages and ages,' he said. 'I've eaten all the chocolate and I've got bored waiting.' Then he saw ZE3. 'Oh, goody! Is he coming to live with us?'

'Yes. He's going to sit in our garden and stare all day long and do absolutely nothing.'

They told him what had happened to Gribble and the other garden gnomes.

'But I don't understand,' Theo said. 'Why was Gribble called Beanpole?'

'It's a joke, Theo. Beanpoles are tall and thin and he is short and fat.'

'Oh, I see. Like calling you Wizard Brain, Joe? Or Laurie, Prince Charming?'

'No, not really – oh, very funny. Ha, ha, I don't think.'

'This was your fault, you know, Theo,' Laurie said. 'If Clinky Monkey didn't wear that diamond collar we'd never have had a garden gnome trying to steal it.'

'But he *does* wear a diamond collar,' Theo said.

'Yes, but—'

'And he is the Cleverest Dog in the World, so he has to have a diamond collar,' Theo said. 'Doesn't he?'

The garden gnome winked in agreement.